THE ELUSIVE PLAYBOY

A Short Story Series

Volume 1

by Thurston Edwards

Copyright © 2024

All rights reserved.

No part of this publication may be reproduced, distributed, or transmitted in any form or by any means, including photocopying, recording, or other electronic or mechanical methods, without the prior written permission of the publisher, except in the case of brief quotations embodied in critical reviews and other noncommercial uses permitted by copyright law.

Table of Contents

Chapter 1 1

Chapter 2 3

Chapter 3 7

Chapter 4 9

Chapter 5 11

Chapter 6 13

Chapter 7 17

Chapter 8 21

Chapter 9 23

Chapter 10 29

Chapter 1

He was sitting at his usual cafe in the 12th Arrondissement of Paris, sipping at a double espresso, flicking nonchalantly through the newspaper, glancing about him, noting who and what was about him. He noted a small flock of pigeons bobbing their heads in random abandon in the middle of the square. A young woman elegantly rode past on her traditional bicycle, complete with wicker basket in the front. An elderly couple, arm in arm, were hobbling slowly across the square, endearingly. Like a couple of tortoises. They occasionally muttered something unintelligible to each other for reassurance. And two men, maybe in their fifties, were gesticulating with angry gestures at each other. Probably about last night's football.

It was a late April afternoon. The air was ever so slightly chilled, and a whiff of the bakery's latest offering came wafting from diagonally opposite the cafe. Sunshine sporadically filled the square for long enough to warm the faces of those seated outside, before cloud snatched it away in an instant, and some decided it was time to go home.

But this wasn't about Paris. Or the weather. This was about the man who was always watching. Noticing. Analysing. Simultaneously noticeable, and forgettable in an instant. When he was sitting still, it was easy to miss him. But when he moved, people watched.

Chapter 2

He had been in Paris a week this time, so far. He flitted around Europe mostly. Businessman they said. Others said criminal. A few even claimed assassin. But what he was, was someone different. It was clear to the waitress who started only last week.

When it came to the man paying his bill, he uttered, "L'addition, s'il vous plait." He then briefly said something to the immaculately dressed lady on the table next to him. And it was over in an instant. Yet the effect on the woman lasted much longer. And the waitress could see it. What did he say?! The lady had transformed instantaneously into a little schoolgirl despite being probably sixty in age. And yet if you'd not looked in their direction for those mere twenty seconds you'd have missed it completely, and wondered why the lady was blushing and laughing to herself a full five minutes later.

The waitress had to find out more about this mysterious man. She took the bill over to him and didn't know why her knees started to fail, and her hands started to shake. Was it because of what she had just seen, and she was nervous of what he might say to her? Or what he might make her feel? She noticed that that feeling, whatever it was, grew in significant strength as she got closer and closer until finally she said, "Bonjour, l'addition pour monsieur." He replied in French but she wasn't listening. She just looked at him. He had sunglasses on so she couldn't see his eyes, but she could feel them piercing into her. He wore a light blue shirt, an emerald green wool vest over the top and black jeans. He was caucasian, but he was unmistakably quite tanned. The kind of tan that suggested he had just been on holiday, or that he was permanently on one. He was probably around forty years old, max forty five. He smiled at her warmly, and she felt physically hugged by it somehow. He then lifted up his glasses to look at her properly, and her heart skipped a beat. She took in a short, sharp breath and did her damnedest to maintain an even countenance.

His eyes were an enchanting mix of blue, green, grey and yellow. The mix was so intense, and so muddled, that they appeared to be morphing at the very moment she peered deeply into them. As if his eye colour was in a constant state of flux and perpetual motion. They were the most beautiful eyes she had ever seen, and everything else to the left, right and in every direction, ceased to exist in that moment. She was transfixed, and trying desperately to conceal it. As she squirmed and hopped from one foot to the other, clenching her fist in the hand that didn't hold the card machine.

Time stood still. The pigeons didn't exist. The bright sun and fluffy clouds didn't exist. The kids running around screaming delight couldn't be heard. Her heartbeat could though. Thump...thump. Through her chest. The only other time she could hear her heartbeat like this was when she had just been on a run and was seriously out of breath. Or in a difficult exam.

She felt like he was toying with her, holding her in his forcefield, forbidding her to leave. He wasn't mean or cruel with this, he just did it naturally. Almost as if he was a natural born hypnotist. And it had only been ten seconds at the most.

He smiled at her with an unmistakably devil-may-care, cheeky smile, and she smiled nervously back. *He must have been able to tell I was uncomfortable as hell*, the waitress thought. The lady on the table nearby had noticed the effect he was having on her as well, and she smiled warmly at the waitress. As if to say, "I understand how you're feeling and there's no shame in it. He did the same to me."

He paid by adroitly tapping his card, and looked up at the waitress again whilst still holding his sunglasses up on his forehead with one hand. The waitress said thank you, and quickly left the time warp she was stuck in. She broke into a little skip, anxious as she was to regain her composure and regain her control. As she reached the inside of the cafe she exhaled deeply and looked flushed. Her manager noticed and rolled his eyes patronisingly at her. Then swiftly told her to see to the new family of four who had sat down ten minutes ago, that no one had served.

Chapter 3

The waitress went home at 6pm after her shift was over, cycling the twenty minute journey home much quicker than usual. Anxiety travelled with her, along with deep yearnings she'd never experienced before. What had that man done to her today? She was only nineteen and she hadn't had that much experience with men. A par for the course teenage romance, and a couple of fumbles here and there. Nothing to write home about. She'd only had sex twice in fact, and both times it was awful.

The first time she was in so much pain that it was impossible for her to enjoy it. And the second time it was with the boy she used to ride bikes around her neighbourhood with as kids. She knew he'd been keen for as long as they'd known each other, and one night she just let him have his way - finally. Although 'his way 'was to struggle to get it in for five minutes, then ejaculating after about forty five seconds. Was this what sex was like? She didn't think about it for more than a few seconds as sex wasn't a priority. Working in a cafe while studying at university, was. She was a responsible girl from a responsible and sober family, after all.

One would describe her as an averagely attractive young woman in her prime age, and she had had hundreds of men make passes at her since she was 14. She wasn't stunningly beautiful by any means, but she had an innocence that men sniffed out. She had been unable to hide it due to her very sheltered upbringing. That and her introversion, which she'd suffered since birth. Though she was quite comfortable in it. Thus despite being of average appearance, her innocence and immaturity made her a flame to which certain men flocked.

As she stared out of her window that night at the Parisian skyline, she found herself lingering in her thoughts, which was unusual. Typically she pushed away any feelings she had, too timid to deal with them. She would distract herself as quickly as she could. Even if it was to do something tedious like line up her books in height order for the hundredth time. A new feeling was present in her. She wasn't sure entirely what it was. It was curiosity mixed with yearning, longing. But for what? She didn't know what she was longing for, but her loins did.

Chapter 4

The next day the waitress cycled to work uneasily. She usually cycled to work in a carefree manner, as it was something she could focus solely on, and forget any of her anxieties. She was in the zone when she cycled, weaving expertly through traffic and pedestrians, sometimes humming or whistling as she went. Today there was no humming. No whistling. And she even got flustered by the Parisian traffic. She finally heard the car's beeps like the cacophony they were in reality.

Upon arriving she wheeled her bike to the back of the cafe where the bikes were kept with the bins, along with a generous amount of pigeon shit, and breathed a sigh of relief that *he* wasn't there. Strange for her to be relieved he wasn't there, when deep down if she admitted it to herself, she hoped he *was* there.

She started at midday and the cafe already had seated its regulars, and those wanting to stop for a quick coffee then bustled on their way. The odd tourist of course stopped by, often to ask for directions to the Eiffel Tower, which always amused the staff. Follow that massive thing in the sky! How they laughed with each other.

By 3pm the cafe was humming away with conversations, and the waitress was beginning to fully relax. She had forgotten all about the man from yesterday. Maybe it was all a dream anyway. Yes…it was a dream…and it didn't really happen, she consoled herself with.

Five o'clock rolled around and the cafe courtyard was sparsely populated. Only four customers remained, and it was eerily quiet in the square for a May afternoon. The waitress took ten minutes to sit and have a coffee herself. She felt quite serene now, and her anxiety and unsettling feelings had fully subsided from earlier that morning. She let out a long exhale and opened her book up to sneak in a few pages before the manager gave her the look that said she had to clean something, somewhere - anything...

A man was walking past the cafe with a woman, arm in arm, laughing wildly and ostentatiously. Everyone in that moment looked up to stare at them accusingly. How could this arrogant couple enjoy themselves so much when this was a quiet space for reflection and melancholic thoughts. You know, the famous French pastime. The waitress looked up and it was *him*...

Her heart stopped and if she had to talk in that moment to save her skin she would have perished. Her throat tightened like a vice, and her hands failed to hold her coffee cup steadily, spilling large parts of it on the table. They'd stopped laughing for now, but were talking animatedly as they walked along the little cobblestoned avenue. The man glanced over his shoulder and caught the waitress looking at him. He smiled a big, knowing, cheeky smile as if to say, "I see you...I know you're looking...you can't resist me...can you?" He winked at her almost imperceptibly, and they bounced along and drifted out of view.

The waitress blushed, caught her breath and attempted to remain composed despite her cheeks reddening, her hands trembling, and the unavoidable fact that she'd forgotten who she was, and where she was. Her manager glared accusingly at her, as if to say out loud: "why on God's green earth do I employ you?!" She blinked several times, shook her head vigorously and did an abrupt about turn; and walked indoors as quickly as her legs would carry her.

Chapter 5

She lamented how the day had been so uneventful and calm; but now she felt that if someone had asked her to tie her own shoelaces, or add two and two, she would fail miserably. She went red again, at the imagined embarrassment. This made her blush yet further with anger at her idiocy. Her shift only had an hour to go after this cataclysmic event, and it went by uneventfully. She served people, smiled apologetically, did her manager's bidding, stared into space; and wondered about the man the rest of the time. She had developed a new habit of shaking her head with gusto, as if to forcibly shake herself out of her stupor. It had a positive effect, so she kept doing it from time to time. What didn't help was her boss kept seeing her do it, and thought she might be insane, as well as inept at her job. She wasn't inept at her job, but the manager was a typically miserable Parisian man, criticising everything and everyone as a force of habit. He probably went home and criticised his wife too, if he was fortunate enough to have one.

The waitress finished cleaning the tables, the floor, stacked the chairs away and counted the money in the till. Then she cycled home the usual way. She felt calm. Or calmer. Normality had been restored somewhat. An equilibrium. As she got home she kicked her shoes off, put her feet up, and watched whatever rubbish was on the telly. She would sometimes allow reality T.V to fill her screen, for which she detested herself for. She knew it was deadening her sharp mind, but she just didn't care after a hard day's work. She made some risotto for dinner, and got an early night.

Then got into bed with her lover - her latest book - a romantic thriller which had some racy passages in it on occasion. She again, as a bookish and slightly reserved young woman, hated herself for liking such smut, but it sated a longing in her to be sexually dominated. She would never admit it to herself, but she craved an older man.

Chapter 6

The next day was a uni day, and she didn't have to worry about seeing the man again. She was studying the history of art at the prestigious Sorbonne university. Her father hated that she was studying something so 'fluffy' to him, but she adored learning about art, and anything to do with it. And besides, she wasn't going to study business or something as odious as that!

She took the metro to the campus as it was further away than the cafe. She enjoyed the anonymity of the metro - hundreds of people just staring into space, or their phones, and she could surreptitiously observe any interesting folk near her. On this day a woman of about seventy-five-years-old caught her eye. She was wearing a bright pink suit, a light blue hat with a feather, and an expression that said "I couldn't give a damn what any of you think of me, I'm as happy as can be." *If only I could have that confidence now, let alone at that age*, she wondered. *Why am I so awkward?! I can't even say hello to people I know without feeling like I'm going to break into a thousand pieces!*

As she mindlessly peered around the carriage…she saw *him*. He was sitting reading a newspaper, looking more serious than she had ever seen him look. The other two times he was in his element entertaining women, being cheeky, arrogant and playful. *Is it actually him?* She thought. *He didn't even have a woman with him.* She gulped, went red and turned the other way in case he saw her.

Staring at her feet for a minute or so her mind was racing along like a madman in a padded cell. What should she do? What should she not do? Should she say hi? Look at him? Flirt with him? Ignore him? Stand near him and hope he says hello?! After two minutes of toing and froing, she resolved to take a risk and move closer to him in the hope that he at least sees her.

As she did this a man sat opposite was staring at her, and she immediately imagined he knew precisely what she was thinking; so she blushed and became angry with herself. *Stop looking at me creep!* She said with her eyes. He grinned at her, and she threw three mental daggers in his direction. He didn't care. She took a breath and walked ten feet towards where the man was sitting, and stood opposite him, slightly to his diagonal left. He didn't even look up from his paper, totally absorbed in the article he was reading. *Bugger*, she thought. *What do I do now?! This is already way beyond my comfort zone,* she riled inside. She desperately attempted to look casual and cool, and lent against the glass by the end seat, showed her legs in the best possible way from his angle, and did her best moody but sexy face, looking down and occasionally swishing her hair and looking wistfully into space, half in his direction. She didn't know where these 'moves 'came from as she'd never even done them before. Ever. But it was what instinct, and bad rom com films had taught her.

Eventually he looked up, and looked to his left past her, then to his right away from her. *He didn't see me! Damn. What do I do? What am I doing?!* Then suddenly she dropped her purse - on purpose - before she knew what she was doing. It made a loud thud, and she acted all flustered and picked it up in a hurry, going red in the process. The man glanced up for a second to see what the kerfuffle was about, as one does when there's a loud noise near you on public transport. It was a look born of instinct, not of desire. But the waitress had desire. And her desire had turned her into a quivering mess, unable to control her actions and behave as she normally would otherwise.

She glanced in his direction as she stood up straight again, swiping away her hair from her face. It was a quick-as-a-flash glance but he caught it, and glanced back. Then he smiled cheekily as if to say *I saw your fumble and it's cute you'd be so uncoordinated.* She blushed and averted his gaze. He smiled to himself, but still looked in her direction and she looked again for a second longer this time. And now as she locked eyes with him she felt a rush of excitement and nervousness. She racked her brain as to what to do next. All she did though was go blank, and frozen. He took another quick look at her up and down, surveying her figure a little more. He didn't object to what he was seeing at least, it seemed to her. He could sense a naïveté and innocence about her, not to mention her unmistakable awkwardness. He found it quite alluring in a primal, predatory way. *She could be easy prey - easy meat.* These thoughts flashed through his mind as the waitress 'thoughts were so jumbled she couldn't have told you what one of them was if a gun was held to her head. She glanced again in his direction, obviously trying to pretend she wasn't checking him out. She'd look past him in a pretence that she didn't even notice him at all. He seemed to smile to himself, and at the girl. Not that she'd dare look at him.

The train stopped at the next stop and the man got up, sauntered towards her, smiled cheekily, and deftly placed a business card in her hand and confidently walked off. She nearly died of embarrassment, excitement and nervousness - all at the same time. It was about ten seconds before she breathed again. *I did it! I got his number!* She was ecstatic. She couldn't believe she had faced her fears and got success. Even if she was dreadfully embarrassed and going to have to go and hide in her bedroom for the next twelve hours just to calm down.

Chapter 7

The business card had faint writing on it: his name, a phone number and his email address. He was stated as being: "Ex-military Entrepreneur". And his name was stated as: Alexander Lovejoy. She gushed. He knew how to kill a man, and probably had. And he was an entrepreneur so he was a risk taker. She loved his name too - it made her fall for him even more. It was a sexy name that suited him so well. *Oh god he's even hotter than I thought...*she mused to herself. *But what do I do now?!*

She decided to send him a text and wait. She agonised for four hours on what to say and eventually sent: "Hi it's the awkward phone fumbler from the metro earlier. I assumed you wanted me to text you. How's your day been?" It was a bit banal, boring and awkward in itself. At least she included a joke of sorts. But she was far too nervous, and her overthinking showed.

She found herself online on and off for the next two hours, praying he would read it. But also praying that he didn't see her online waiting like the desperate teenager she was behaving as. Or maybe she still was, in her mind at least. Eventually he did read it, four hours after she sent it. He read it and didn't reply. Her mind now raced at a thousand miles an hour with thoughts such as, *"why did I write that?"* And: *"He must think I'm so dull. He's never going to reply. Why am I so stupid?! I should never have made that ridiculous performance on the metro. Ahhh!"* She screamed into her pillow at home. The uncertainty and insecurity reaching inordinate proportions.

But then he did reply. At 11:36 pm that night. He wrote: "Hi 'phone fumbler'. Cute name. I'm out late tonight, come grab a drink now. I'm in the bar opposite your cafe in the square. I'll be here until 12:30 am." She stopped breathing and sat quickly down on her kitchen chair, staring at the message. "Come grab a drink now." It stared at her and she stared back. She hoped that by staring at it a decision would miraculously be made, and she would be out the door and on her way. But all she could think was how could she meet him this late? *And what about the fact I won't have time to wash my hair and do my makeup properly. And what the fuck do I wear?!* Twenty minutes went by while she thought like this. She would have to throw some clothes on and get a taxi in the next fifteen minutes if she was to make the 12:30 am deadline.

She did just that. Threw on some clothes - some old jeans that made her bum look good, a top that showed a little cleavage and a cardigan in case it was chilly. She sprayed perfume all over her neck and top as if she was attempting to bathe in it, skipped out the door and ordered a taxi online as she bustled down the stairs breathlessly.

The taxi arrived within four minutes, and she slumped into the back seat and chewed on her nails ferociously. Her thoughts kept bouncing around her skull like a crazed pinball. One appeared as instantaneously as the next appeared. She didn't exchange a word with the taxi driver as she normally would. Polite conversation would have been the norm, but she was so focussed on meeting this mysterious man that she didn't care for pleasantries. She arrived close by, checked her hair in the window as she exited and at least managed to utter: "au revoir".

Gulping as she walked, she peered over to the bar where she hoped he still was. It was 12:19 am and she was about seventy metres from the bar. Around thirty tables were still positioned outside, but roughly only ten customers were using them. Then she noticed *him*. He was sat ostentatiously on a small table by himself, sipping from a large glass on what looked to be red wine. His left arm was outstretched, hanging over the chair to his left. His right hand picked up and put the glass of red down on the table carelessly. He still had his shades on despite it being after midnight. *Who does he think he is?!* The waitress thought.

She took a deep breath in and approached his table with purpose, despite her wanting the ground to swallow her right there so she didn't have to go through with actually meeting him. As she reached to be within ten feet of him, he must have felt her presence as he turned slightly and smirked in her direction. "You made it…and just in time!" He said to her brashly. She blushed, and hated herself for it. "Hi…" was all she could muster as she sat down opposite him.

"Glad you made it. I wasn't sure if you were a spontaneous girl or not. Seems you are." He winked at her and she blushed again, going went bright red. "It's ok I won't bite…" He continued. She wanted him to bite her though. He could do anything to her. She'd let him bend her over the table right here if they could get away with it.

"What would you like to drink?" He offered. "A vodka lemon and lime please." She said politely back, as if he was her teacher, or grandfather. He was definitely older, maybe twice her age. Yet they were both adults; so nothing massively out of the ordinary really. "Nice choice. Classy lady I see." He kept grinning mischievously at her, which left her unnerved. The drink came and she drank it like she would a glass of water - in about three minutes. Her nerves were calmed and she felt the first wave of a tiny bit of confidence swell inside her. Or maybe just a bit of relief that she wasn't going to feel terrified the *whole time* with him.

"So how about we blow this joint and go for a walk by the Seine?" He expressed this as more of an order than a question, and she wasn't going to object. She left like a schoolgirl with a strict teacher. She certainly didn't feel she had any power or right to object to anything he said. "Sure," was all she managed as she meekly got up from the table and waited for him to pay the bill. He flirted with the waitress - of course - and then strolled over to her smiling from ear to ear, as the most suave man she had ever met.

Chapter 8

They soon reached the riverside and were making idle conversation. He asked her about her life, her family and the usual things. She replied with short replies and had never felt so unsure of herself with a man before. She would usually have been at least a little confident. About ten minutes passed and he started to playfully nudge her and touch her gently in all sorts of ways. He was breaking down the invisible barriers between them - she was none the wiser to this predator's tactics.

He abruptly grabbed her elbow, stopping her and asked: "What do you dream about for your future?" She laughed nervously and started to answer by saying: "Well I want to finish my degree and then I'd really like to…" As she was awkwardly getting the words out he placed his right hand delicately on the left side of her face and gently pulled her towards him, looked deeply into her eyes and kissed her passionately. It only lasted three seconds, but it was the best kiss she had ever had by a country mile. She felt a tingle all over and wanted more, but he had already retreated from her and gone back to his listening pose, informing her to "Continue…"

But she couldn't think …and he had to remind her of what she had been saying. Eventually she regained some level of composure, yet all she could think about was that kiss. He left her wanting more. So much more. And he knew it.

Now she crept closer to him as they walked, accidentally bumping into him repeatedly. She brushed his shoulder, his arm, and even pretended to trip up and have him catch her 'fall'. He grinned it seemed - constantly. He was having the time of his life being cheeky and mischievous. While she was floundering, treading water, just trying to keep up mentally with his sharp wit and savvy mind.

They reached another bridge and he led her to the middle, gently touched the small of her back and pulled her abruptly to him and kissed her hard. It was harder this time and he lent his body firmly against hers. This time he kissed her for a good thirty seconds and stopped, looked her in the eyes and said: "Let's go to my place." And, like the obedient schoolgirl she was, she followed him the two streets to his front door. He deftly opened the building door with a fob, led her inside and up the two flights of stairs to his front door. He said absolutely nothing during this time. He simply held her right hand tightly in his left, as he led her on a merry dance to his apartment. She merely followed, utterly submissively.

Chapter 9

His front door opened to a gorgeously presented but minimalistic apartment, with a view to the Eiffel tower, and a classical Parisian skyline. He had green plants at regular intervals around the living room, and a very impressive bookcase filled with at least two hundred books. The sofa was large, wide and irresistibly inviting. He motioned her to the kitchen where he poured them both a glass of red wine without asking if she in fact wanted a glass. He sipped at it greedily - like an animal would drink blood - and told her to savour it as it was a very expensive bottle. Or so he said. She couldn't be sure if it was part of his game. She felt as if she was in a whirlwind, losing all control of her body, her senses…her actions. He was her master and she was putty he could mould into any shape he wanted. Resistance would not only be futile, but impossible.

They had a few sips in the kitchen, with him only muttering a few things about how great the wine was. Barely two minutes had gone by before he nudged her in the direction of the living room. The waitress allowed herself to be nudged, and had to stop herself from running over to the sofa and laying on it, legs spread. Instead she slowed herself down and waited for him to tell her where to sit, as if she was in detention. He sat on the sofa and told her to come sit next to him. Duly, she did and they continued to make smalltalk. And by smalltalk I mean he talked, and she listened and smiled at what she was hoping were the right moments. She was so terrified to speak that when she did a squeak came out first, and then, if she was lucky, a few coherent words. *Are we going to kiss? Have sex? Does he fancy me or am I just a toy to cure his boredom for an evening? Something to play with. Maybe he felt sorry for me and just wanted to give me some adult company and some fun away from work. Maybe he just saw me as a...friend!*

She turned away in an attempt to hide the panic and horror of her anxiety filled thoughts. As she half turned back to face him, his face was suddenly three inches away from hers, and he kissed her before she could breathe. Catching her breath she moved away a few inches, just to try to understand what was happening. He allowed only a second of this before he leaned into her again and hovered an inch from her face. She could feel his hot, heaving breath on her face and his lips were moist and glistening in the moonlight, filtering in through the windows and the unused curtains. He stared intently at her with his liquid eyes, and she hadn't the strength to avert his gaze. She was in his portal. His vortex. His power. He moved his face an inch closer to hers so his lips were irresistibly close to hers. Tantalising her. Teasing her. And she was breathless. Time stood still and she'd never been so frozen and turned on at the same time in her life. Nothing even close to this. It was shocking to her that she could be so frozen mentally, yet so wet at the same time. She was afraid he would feel her down there and be put off by the river that was gushing out of her. *He's only kissed me so far!*

He removed his sweater and revealed a tight navy blue - or black - she couldn't tell - t-shirt that hugged his torso quite tightly. He was strong and toned, but not muscular. She caught a glimpse of his arms out the corner of her eye as she was kissing him and her river continued to run even more freely. *If there was a dam up inside me, it had definitely burst.*

He had nudged her deftly onto her back; onto the wide, luxurious sofa now and he was writhing all over her, kissing her with his carnal desire. He alternated between kisses all up and down her neck, and her soft lips. Sometimes he just breathed hot air onto her neck, and she heaved with animal thirst. Her back was arching so considerably that it looked like an impossible position to be in. Or that she was doing some kind of impossible yoga pose.

As he undid the first button he looked up at her, ceasing the feverish kissing for a second. He wanted to pause before he truly devoured his prey. He wanted his prey to know he was completely in control and there was no escape now. The glint in his eye, however, reassured her that this was all good, clean fun. Or perhaps not so clean. She bit her own lip and he undid another button, and another, and revealed her young, pert bosoms, nestling beneath her brassiere. He kissed the top of her breasts and slowly made his hands up her side until he reached her breasts. He grabbed them firmly and kneaded them like dough, pushing them against her ribs, passionately yet firmly. Then, still kissing her neck, he used the first two fingers on his right hand to peel back the top of the bra on her left side, revealing her left nipple. It was soft but fully erect and he squeezed it. She moaned and gasped simultaneously. He pulled down on the other side of the bra to reveal the right nipple. He squeezed this one too, a little harder and she yelped out loud. It hurt a little, but it was good pain. Pausing he looked at her again with those liquidly seductive eyes and pounced on her nipples with his mouth, biting the nipples hard, and licking them afterwards. Much like a cat would its owner's hand, after it playfully bit it.

She was wide-eyed and ten times more turned on than she'd ever been at the point. He then delicately reached around to her back and removed the clasp of her bra with one hand. This wasn't something she even thought a man was capable of doing. Her bosoms felt cool in the night air and the breeze drafting through the window made them tingle yet further. Her nipples had never been so erect in her life, she didn't know they could grow to be this long and this hard. He was licking and squeezing and biting her nipples now, and her knickers and jeans were so soaked she couldn't believe he hadn't noticed as yet. *Or maybe he had?* As if he had heard her thoughts, he reached down and felt the wet patch spanning several inches across, where her crotch was, and her jeans still clung to her legs. He grinned and said with his now trademark wink: "Is there a river down there or something?" She blushed and said: "I guess there is…"

The animal joy with which he proceeded was mesmerising in its power and majesty. She couldn't help but observe all his movements with reverence, powerlessness and no less admiration. He was in control but she was allowing him that control. There was no issue of consent here. And he wasn't even being rough with her, just dominant and powerful. Masterful even. She realised in that moment that she was submissive, and she liked dominant men. This basic but pivotal basis for her personality was hidden from her until this man, Alexander Lovejoy, awakened it in her.

Whilst this brief reverie went on, he had unbuttoned the top button of her jeans, unzipped the fly, and was now yanking at her tight denim jeans from first her thigh and then near her ankle. He did it with wild abandon, frustration even that it took so long. Relieving her of the jeans he looked satisfied and he grinned at her devilishly. She half-smiled back, excited but nervous for him to feel how wet she was.

His right gently caressed her left knee and slowly, deliberately he ran his fingers up her inner thigh while kissing her softly this time. He had changed speeds and she felt this was now 'tease mode'. Upon reaching four or so inches from her knickers, he felt the first bit of her moisture on her inner thigh. His eyes widened almost imperceptibly, and he continued on up the thigh and reached the knickers themselves. If a doctor checked for her breathing at this moment, he would have found no sign of life.

Instead of continuing up and finally touching her x rated place, he got to the edge of her knickers and stopped. This really was 'tease mode'. It made a difference from the guy who ejaculated in the first thirty seconds! His left hand now clutched her knee lovingly, and slowly he stroked his fingers up her inner thigh whilst kissing her neck this time. She was sighing deeply and moaning moans that came from so deep within her, she wasn't conscious of them happening. His fingers slowly lingered on her thigh and inched closer, inch by inch, up her thigh to her knickers. The last few inches were of course lubricated with her moistness, so he momentarily slipped and he was finally touching her dripping pussy.

He deftly rubbed it up and down vertically at first, feeling for all its contours. He pressed a little firmer and her legs got wider, as her hips burned with the strain of being positioned so open as never before. She moaned and groaned, her eyes shut at this point. As he continued to rub and feel just how wet she was, it was then he finally did it. He pulled the side of her knickers to one side and slipped a finger into her pussy so suddenly, the waitress screamed. What had felt like an eternity for him to finally touch her *there*, was in fact probably no more than five minutes. She writhed her body side to side, and moaned louder than she ever had done. Even the thought of others hearing her screams in the apartments below and above didn't matter to this typically shy and reserved girl.

One finger suddenly became two…he now used both to pleasure her. She had never been fingered in such a sensual and powerful way before. Not even close. *I can't believe this feels so good…how is he doing this to me?!* He continued alternating speeds, locations and occasionally took them out to tease the surrounding areas, dripping with her wetness, teasing her for a few seconds near her opening, before driving them inside her again, right to the very back of his reach. She gasped, moaned and arched her back all at the same time. He did this again but this time focussing gently on her clitoris, which he knew *exactly* the location of. He alternated between stimulating the clitoris and sliding his finger so deep…*I think I'm gonna come oh god!*

She came ferociously, and her entire body shuddered under the guttural release. His hand was covered in her fluid and he grinned that grin of his as if to say 'I knew that would happen and I'm used to it.' Her arch back finally slumped back onto the sofa and she only then realised her back and torso were covered in sweat. Not only were her inner thighs dripping wet, but her whole body was encased in sweat beads. *I must have lost a couple of pounds in the last twenty minutes! I needed to lose a bit of weight.*

She was exhausted, mentally and physically. He looked a little worn out himself. She could see sweat covering his forehead and his t-shirt had multiple sweat patches. As she wondered what might happen next, he got up and briskly went over to the kitchen. She heard the fridge open and then liquid being poured. He coughed a couple of times to clear his throat and she could hear him gulping liquid down. A few seconds later he came back carrying two big glasses of water.

Chapter 10

"Figured you'd need this," he winked, smiling. He had the peculiar ability of making everything he did sexual, without even trying. She was already getting turned on again when he said, "You ok to get home? I've got an early start tomorrow. Hopping on a plane." She didn't hide her surprise or her disappointment at all, replying, "Oh...ok...where you off to?"

"Africa."

"Oh...ok. You ever come back to Paris much?" She was being unusually unreserved and direct, surprising herself. He grinned, again.

"I do come back here quite a bit, yeah. I like the women here." He winked and laughed straight after. She laughed and blushed straight after.

"Will I see you again?" She said trying not to sound desperate, only half-succeeding. He laughed again, this time for several seconds.

"Maybe." He winked again, and then made himself busy organising stuff in the living room and the kitchen. *I better get dressed then, he seems to want to get rid of me.* He turned to her as he put some plates in his dishwasher, saying,

"You sure you're ok to get home?" *Was this a test? Was he offering to take me home?*

"Oh yeah sure, no problem. I'll order a taxi now on my phone. Be here in a couple of minutes." He nodded, closing the dishwasher door and pressing for it to begin.

"Great. Nice spending time with you. Enjoy yourself?!" He laughed but smiled warmly at her, indicating a glimpse of his inner world perhaps for the first time. It was as if he knew she was feeling insecure at that moment, and wanted to reassure her. She wasn't sure how much warmth he had to add to his ragingly overt sexuality until that moment. Apparently a little, at least…maybe. It was too fleeting to read too much into.

She made her way towards the door, finishing off getting dressed as she did. She didn't want to outstay her welcome, after all. Sitting on the chair by the door, putting on her boots she looked up at him as he was moving around the flat, tidying up. His toned body was hidden beneath his t-shirt still, and she longed to see what was underneath it. Not to mention what was in his trousers. He moved so effortlessly, gliding, swaggering movements…and animalistically. Sexiness oozed off him in spades that it was hard to believe he could walk down a street in Paris without making at least one woman faint, or become severely turned on just by seeing him for a few seconds.

"All good?" he remarked casually, still moving around.

"Yep, guess I'll be off then." She went to open his door to let herself out, desperately lingering as long as she possibly could without it being weird. *I don't want to leave!* She turned around to say a final farewell and he was there right behind her all of a sudden.

"Couldn't let you go without a goodnight kiss, could I?" He smiled, grabbed her by the waist and pulled her against his body hard. Then kissed her passionately for maybe three seconds, pushed her away and said,

"Get home safe now," and closed the door with a final grin.

She was outside in the cool stairwell, faced with three levels of stone staircase to descend. She didn't even remember climbing them. *Did I fly up here?* As she slowly walked down the steps, one by one, she felt a lightness, almost giddiness descend over here. Something inside her had shifted. *But why didn't he sleep with me?* She kept asking herself that question all the way home, and for the next few weeks, hoping he might appear at her cafe again, grinning at her.

Printed in Great Britain
by Amazon